About the Book:

CHILDREN OF FAMOUS AMERICANS BOOK -
Annie Lee and the Wooden Skates
By Margaret Friskey, illustrated by
Darrell Wiskur.

There are seven Lee children who live
in a big mansion ... surrounded by a
dark forest and the treacherous Potomac
River. In their carefree way, with
seven horses, eleven cats, a pony and
a stray dog, they romp through this warm-
hearted story. Annie, whose attempts
at skating are no better than her other
skills, discovers something more impor-
tant than performance.

CP price to schools & libraries - $2.96

CHILDRENS PRESS
1224 West Van Buren St.
Chicago, Illinois 60607

D1529354

ANNIE LEE AND THE WOODEN SKATES

Annie Lee
AND THE WOODEN SKATES

By Margaret Friskey

Illustrations by Darrell Wiskur

CHILDRENS PRESS, CHICAGO

CONTENTS

1 THE FIRST DANCE

"You mean to say you got that dog in here again, Miss Annie?" Amanda swept into Annie's room at Arlington and set her candle down on the chest of drawers. She glared at Spec curled up before the bedroom fire. She looked as though she were thinking of dropping him in the well.

Amanda was lean and dark and troubled. Her face loomed up like a thundercloud between the snowy bandanna on her head and the white shawl collar of her dress. Her long, yellow calico skirt was gathered into a tight waistband. Its stiff, starched folds reached toward the floor as though ready on a moment's notice to support her if her legs gave out. They never did.

Amanda could keep the household at Arlington running smoothly. She could see that wood was

brought in for the countless fireplaces, and that the
dark floors were polished, and that the silver shone,
and that the cooking proceeded as it should. . . .
But the Lee children!

They had seven riding horses and a pony, and
eleven cats. They had the freedom to roam through
the six hundred acres of dark forest behind the
house. They frequently sailed on the treacherous
Potomac River which flowed in front of Arlington.
The Lee children were the source of constant con-
cern to Amanda.

"Dogs no more belong in a lady's bedroom than
pigs in the parlor." Amanda folded back the counterpane with its popcorn tufts of candlewicking,
and tucked the blanket in around Annie.

"He's beautiful!" said Annie. Although she was
eight years old, she looked very tiny sitting in the
middle of the big bed. A bed so big and high she had
to climb up a little pair of steps to get into it.

"Looks more like a hank of wool that the moths
had been at," answered Amanda.

Spec busily polished the floor with his short tail.
His quiet eyes followed Amanda around the room,
but not with fear.

Amanda had been storming about his presence
ever since Robert E. Lee had found him half-
drowned in the narrows of the river and brought
him to Annie. That was last fall. The last English
ship, the *Bonnie Bristol*, with Captain Donahue at

the wheel, had just sailed down the river carrying a load of tobacco to England.

Now the ice was gone from the river. The redbud and the dogwood were in bloom.

"I wish I weren't just in between," said Annie.

"Between what, honey, the sheets?"

"No, silly. I mean Agnes, Bob, and Mildred are still babies. The nurse puts them to bed, and they go to sleep. And Boo, Mary, and Fitzhugh are almost grown-up. They go downstairs to dance with the company. I'm just in between. And I'm awkward at every grown-up thing I try to do."

"Bless your little heart, child. You're just about right. That you are. All you need to do is just shut your eyes and take four or five deep breaths. You're going to wake up fast asleep. Tomorrow you'll be a whole day older."

Amanda picked up her candle, scowled at Spec and left. Annie could hear her getting bedding from the linen room at the end of the hall to make up beds for the boys on the floor. It often happened when the house was full of cousins that there weren't enough beds to go around.

Finally Annie heard Amanda go down the back stairs. The second floor of Arlington House was dark and quiet.

Annie lay still as a mouse in the big walnut bed with its towering posts and white canopy. This spacious old house in which she lived had already been

11

the home of her Grandma and Grandpa Custis for forty years. Eight-year-old Annie Lee was vaguely aware that the house was steeped in traditions as old as the country.

Grandpa Custis grew up in George Washington's home at Mount Vernon. He was a grandson of Martha Washington. When his father died during the Revolutionary War, George Washington adopted him and his sister Nellie, and they were known as the "children of Mount Vernon."

Grandpa Custis' full name was George Washington Parke Custis. He lived at Mount Vernon from the time he was a baby until he was a young man. After George Washington died, and later Martha Washington, the beautiful house at Mount Vernon was closed. George Washington Parke Custis married a young Virginia beauty. He built Arlington House for his bride on a high bluff just a few miles up the river from Mount Vernon, overlooking the Potomac River and the city of Washington.

The stones used for the house were taken from the land. The bricks were molded from the clay found on the place, and burned in a kiln. The mortar, which held the bricks together, was made by burning oyster shells in a kiln to make lime, which was mixed with sand and water.

Walnut trees were felled and sawed into wide boards and pegged together to make the floors.

It was a grand mansion, impressive as a Greek

temple on a hilltop. Its eight enormous columns, two stories high, which supported the veranda roof, were made of homemade bricks and cemented over to make them perfectly round.

Arlington House had grown from the land as surely as one of the giant pines in the dark forest. It was substantial enough to stand forever.

13

Some of the furniture was brought over from Mount Vernon. Some of it came by sailing ship from England. Much of it was made in the carpenter shop from walnut, pine, and hickory that grew on the place. The rugs, as well as most of the bedding and the clothes, were woven in the weaving house.

George Washington Parke Custis and his wife had a daughter named Mary. When she grew up, she married a tall, handsome graduate of West Point named Robert E. Lee.

Robert E. Lee and his wife, Mary, also made the Arlington mansion their home. This is probably a very good reason why—as the years went by—the seven Lee children made it their home, too.

Eight-year-old Annie felt the enchantment of the place as she lay awake in her bed. There was no shadow yet of the Civil War which would split the country in half and send Robert E. Lee off to serve the Confederate Army as its commander in chief.

Annie didn't take four or five deep breaths and go to sleep as Amanda had suggested. She lay very still with her blue eyes wide open and listened.

She could hear gay voices and laughter down in the drawing room. Soon the little pianoforte began to tinkle a rhythmic tune. Annie knew they were dancing. She wanted to see.

She tossed back her blanket and climbed out of bed. Spec stood up and stretched.

"Sh!" said Annie to him. "Don't make any noise."

The two of them crept into the hall that was lighted by a couple of candles in hurricane chimneys. They went halfway down the stairs, until they could see the dancers.

Annie was entranced. She sat huddled in the corner of the stair, her arm around Spec's neck. She watched for a few minutes with her bare feet keeping time on the wooden step. Suddenly an idea struck her.

She went into her mother's room and put on one of her old dresses. It was very big. The sleeves hung down over her hands. Great folds of the long velvet skirt lay on the floor. The low-cut neck fell off Annie's shoulders exposing a wide expanse of her snow-white nightgown which buttoned up around her throat. She picked up her skirts with a flourish and stepped out into the dimly lighted hall. The music trickled up the stairs.

"Bow," she said to Spec, "and glide ten steps to the right." Spec sat perfectly still with his head cocked to one side.

"You don't seem to get the idea," said Annie. "Some folks never do. You watch me." She locked arms with an imaginary partner and swung around.

"May I have this dance, madam?" A deep voice stopped her in the middle of her twirl. Annie turned around. Her eyes were on a level with the top of her father's head as he bowed solemnly before her, with his hand across his breast.

Annie thought her father was the handsomest man she had ever seen. His black hair curled slightly at the ends. His face was smooth-shaven except for his black mustache. His dark waistcoat was close-fitting and long, and his fawn colored trousers were strapped securely under his shining black boots. He wore a flowing cravat knotted carelessly at his throat.

"Thank you," said Annie, curtsying so low that

her velvet dress rippled into a pool on the dark floor. "I would love to dance with you."

Together they glided the length of the hall and back again.

"You dance divinely, madam," said Annie's tall partner. "Tell me, haven't I met you here before?"

"Oh, its quite unlikely, sir," said Annie with a shy look at her father. "You see, I've only been here eight years."

The candles flickered in their tall chimneys. Spec, watching the dancers, stood up on his hind legs and walked down the middle of the hall.

"Your friend over there is trying a few steps by himself," said Robert Lee. "He looks like a backwoodsman that needs a shave."

"He's no backwoodsman," said Annie in defense of her pet. "He's . . . he's English, and I love him."

"Oh, I see. Well, it just shows that it isn't always grace and charm that win a lady's heart."

Robert Lee with a twinkle in his eyes looked a little puzzled at the white frill of Annie's nightie which showed above her ball gown. Then he leaned down and whispered very confidentially in her ear:

"Pardon me, madam, but your underwear is showing."

"My what . . . oh, ouch!" Annie stopped dancing. She picked up her foot and regarded her big toe intently.

"Barefoot! Mercy on us. Don't you know you'll catch your death of cold, little Ladybug?"

"I only caught a little sliver," said Annie as she plucked it out with her fingernails.

"That is very serious," said her father. "You must get into bed at once." He picked Annie up in his arms and carried her into her room. He dropped her into the middle of her feather bed. Annie crawled out of the top of the green dress and under the covers.

"Robert! Oh, Robert!" It was Annie's mother coming up the stairs.

"Yes, Mary," he replied, slipping the velvet dress under the fold of the counterpane and coming out into the hall.

"Whatever became of you, Robert?" said Annie's mother. "Everyone is asking for you downstairs."

19

"I came up to see if Annie was covered. I was afraid her feet might get cold. There is still a chill in the air, don't you think?"

"Annie's asleep, I suppose," said her mother, turning toward the stairs.

"Like a log," said Robert Lee, as he offered his wife his arm. He started down the stairs with her to join the dancers and play the part of host to all his other guests.

Annie sat up in bed and caught a glimpse of her mother. Mrs. Lee was dressed in a froth of sheer mousseline with a full ruffled skirt. It was ornamented with velvet bows and bouquets of feathers. The sleeves were short and tight and without shoulder straps. Her dark hair hung in long ringlets at the sides of her neck, and the back hair was braided into a figure eight.

Annie thought wistfully of her own straight, corn-colored hair. She reflected rather glumly that it wasn't much good being just in between, especially when you couldn't do any of the things the older children did. Boo and Fitzhugh could ride like Indians and shoot, and make all manner of things in the carpenter shop. Mary, who was twelve, and quite grown-up, had lovely curls and could dance or sit a horse like a queen.

"I can't even dance without getting a sliver in my toe," said Annie into her pillow. Then she took four or five deep breaths and went to sleep.

2 THE UNFINISHED FOX HUNT

The next morning Annie was having her breakfast with the younger children in the small family dining room, just back of the family parlor. Her small feet snuggled cosily side by side on the rag rug beneath the table. Her ruffled pantalets peeked out below the hem of her everyday cotton dress. She had brushed her hair back off her face. A steel spring covered with velvet held it there.

Her father and mother and Grandpa and Grandma Custis and the older children were eating breakfast with the guests at the great round table in the big dining room.

Annie liked the small dining room. She liked the walnut sideboard with its friendly blue plates. She liked the confusion of eating with Agnes who was only five, and Bob who was two and a half and just big enough to feed himself. Millie was a baby in a long white dress with dozens of tucks and rows of lace. Aunt Lucy held her on her broad lap while she looked after Bob who, in his enthusiasm for the business at hand, didn't seem to care whether he piled his breakfast into his mouth or on his shirt.

There was a bowl of flowers on the table from the small conservatory on the southwest corner of the house. One of the things that Grandpa Custis had brought with him from Mount Vernon was George Washington's deep love of flowers. Grandma Custis loved flowers, too. She had a rose garden at the north of the house that was famous throughout Virginia.

The morning air was fragrant with the smell of corn bread, bacon, biscuits and honey, scrambled eggs, and crisp slices of ham. The great trays of food were carried into the house from the summer kitchen out behind the house, where Uncle Ephraim ruled like a king over his domain of big iron kettles and an open fire.

Grandpa Custis stuck his head in the door of the small dining room. His eyes were smiling, and his long white hair was brushed back giving him the distinguished air of a Virginia gentleman. He loved having his beautiful mansion full of grandchildren. They were all aware of this and loved him in return.

"Good morning, children," he said, beaming at them. "You are all looking fit this morning."

"Are they going hunting today?" asked Annie.

"Quails, I believe," Grandpa Custis said. Then he turned and went down the broad hall with one of the guests. It gave him great pleasure to show visitors some of the treasures from Mount Vernon.

"See this iron lantern?" Annie heard him say. "It hung in the hall at Mount Vernon for thirty years. And this was George Washington's porcelain bowl. Beautiful with its gold bands and blue stars, isn't it?" His voice trailed off toward the other end of the house.

"And this was his tea service. It served most of the great men who came to see Washington at Mount Vernon, and some very lovely ladies, too, I might add. . . . But do let me show you the little silver chest that once held a fortune in English money. It belonged to Martha Washington—thirty thousand pounds she had stored in it. . . ." Grandpa Custis needed very little encouragement to talk about his boyhood at Mount Vernon.

"You ain't aiming to go quail hunting, are you, Miss Annie?" asked Amanda, who had come into the dining room and was cutting up a piece of bacon for Bob.

"I haven't got a gun, you know," replied Annie, indirectly.

"It's just as well you don't, replied Amanda.

"Couldn't shoot it if I had one, I suppose," said Annie a little wistfully.

"But you're thinking in there under your yellow hair that you might just ride along with those quail hunters?" Amanda asked.

"Well . . ." Annie was busy trying to catch the honey in a spoon as it dripped off her hot corn bread.

"You're not much bigger than a quail yourself, Miss Annie. You know that. Like as not, somebody is going to shoot you for one and carry you home in their side pocket."

"I think I'll ride Creole," Annie said. "Mary will be riding Lucy Belle."

"Creole!" Amanda's eyes were circles of white in her dark face. "Laws-a-massy. He's a full-sized horse."

"I know." Annie hastened to finish her breakfast.

Amanda went mumbling off toward the summer kitchen. "Ain't fittin'. That's what it ain't."

Annie slipped out of the door. She ran through the rose garden to the stable and had Uncle Daniel saddle Creole for her. He seemed much higher than she remembered him. The sidesaddle wouldn't have been harder to get to if it had been put on the peak of the stable roof.

She led this mountain of horseflesh by its leather reins up to the back steps of the house just as the others came out to get their horses which were saddled and waiting.

Mary was a picture in her new riding habit of bright broadcloth. There were yards and yards of material in the skirt that swirled around her ankles. Her tight jacket buttoned up the front with dozens of jet buttons, two or three of which were left undone to show her white blouse collar which turned down over a checkered scarf. Her hat might have been worn by a Spanish cavalier. All of the girls who were riding that morning wore similar habits. Some of them were red. Some brown. Some of the older girls wore heavy veils on their hats to protect their faces from the sun.

Annie's simple cotton dress and pantalets seemed hopelessly inadequate for the occasion.

Boo came up to her to offer to help her mount. He wore a short tight waistcoat and riding breeches and boots. He was fourteen and almost a man. Boo's real name was Custis, although he was seldom called that.

"Isn't this fellow pretty big for you, Annie?" he asked, taking the reins.

"I'm growing, you know." Down in her heart she doubted it. She was sure she was shrinking every minute, and the horse was growing bigger.

"Of course! I hadn't noticed." Boo rumpled her hair in a friendly gesture. "Look here, young lady, if you are planning to follow this quail hunt you stay back, won't you? And be very quiet."

She put her left foot in the stirrup, and Boo hoisted her up as though she were a feather. She felt smaller than ever perched on Creole's broad back. The big horse tossed his head a couple of times and began to drift sideways across the lawn like a ship that had lost its rudder. Then he began to back up toward the well. For a minute Annie panicked. But finally she managed to get Creole to stand still.

Suddenly Uncle Daniel came running across the drive. "Oh, Mister Boo! Mister Fitzhugh!" he cried.

"What are you so excited about, Uncle Daniel?" asked Fitzhugh. He was a couple of years younger than Mary, and dressed in a dark hunting outfit and leather boots.

"There's a red fox in the south pasture. A red fox,

sir. One of the field hands just came in to tell. Saw him run out of the dark wood and across the field. He's as red as I'm white-headed and all rusted out in my joints," Uncle Daniel declared.

"A red fox! A red fox!" The exciting word flew around. Gray foxes were often seen in the Virginia woods, but a red fox, swift and cunning, was a hunter's gift from heaven.

Annie was forgotten in the excitement. The horsemen quickly galloped out of the drive and off through the woods in the direction of the south pasture. Creole shot forward with the rest. Annie found herself riding hard with the others in the wild pace of a fox hunt. This was something different than quietly routing a covey of quail out of the long grass in the meadow.

There would be fences to jump. Annie had never jumped before, but she couldn't turn back now. What was it she had heard her father tell the boys about jumping? Oh, yes—"Give your horse his head and throw your weight forward as you go over." That would be easy—give Creole his head.

Amanda stood in the driveway until the sound of hooves and barking dogs died away in the distance. Then with a sigh and a shake of her dark head she went back into the house. There was much to be done, for they would all come riding back by noon as hungry as wolves.

The sun rose higher and higher in the sky, and

the strip of river at the foot of the hill sparkled beneath it. Mrs. Lee and the girls who had not ridden on the hunt came out onto the long front veranda to wait for the return of the hunters. Some of them sewed. The others walked up and down; the skirts of their long dimity dresses just missing the bricks of the floor.

Suddenly the noisy riders dashed out of the woods. They whirled up and pulled their horses to a stop in front of the house. They were a hot and happy crowd. Boo flung off his mount and came up on the veranda to present the red, bushy tail of the fox to his favorite cousin from Fairfax County. Everyone teased him, and she blushed the color of the roses in her dress.

Amanda came out through the door. "Where's Miss Annie?" she demanded.

Silence fell. Annie was nowhere to be seen.

"Annie?" said Mrs. Lee. "I haven't seen her all morning."

"I forgot all about her," said Boo. "She was riding Creole."

Just then, Spec began to make a lot of noise out in the back drive. They all ran through the house to see what was the matter. There was Creole trotting quietly toward the stable. His saddle was empty, and his stirrup bumped idly against his side.

Boo ran after Creole and caught his bridle. He whirled the horse around with a jerk.

"You good-for-nothing bundle of bones," he cried. "Where did you dump Annie?" He started toward the road with long strides, leading the horse. When he reached the gate, he saw Annie trudging along in the dust toward home. The side of her dress was dirty; there was a smudge on the side of her nose. In her two hands she was carrying a small furry bundle—a baby squirrel.

Boo lifted her up into the saddle without a word. Then he turned and led Creole back toward the house.

"He must have fallen out of the nest," said Annie. "I'm going to feed it and tame it."

"Look here," said Boo. "What I want to know is what happened to you? Did Creole throw you?"

"Well," said Annie, rubbing the bruise on the side

of her leg, "you know where you went over that first jump?"

"Sure, I know. I'm going to sell this horse and let him pull a canal barge. He ought to be shot."

"Oh, no!" cried Annie in alarm. "He jumped all right. I didn't. Don't you see? I'm kind of little to pull a canal barge . . . but you could shoot me."

"You funny lamb," laughed Boo. "There isn't an animal on all this place that hasn't got you for a friend."

When they reached the porch, Boo helped Annie down off Creole. She was conscious of the excitement she had caused, for everyone was there to see her: the girls in their fresh dimity dresses, and the girls in their fine riding habits with their big hats. There was a babble of voices around her. Suddenly she felt disheveled and awkward.

Annie finally escaped into the house and mounted the stairs slowly, holding the little, warm, throbbing body of the squirrel against her neck.

"I know," she said to him, "I know just how you feel. If we were squirrels instead of the Lees of Arlington, and we had to live in a nest in a tree, and learn to walk along a limb holding on by our toes, everyone could do it except me. I would fall off." She was perfectly sure of it.

The side of her leg ached and her heart was sore. But the little squirrel needed to be taken care of, so she didn't have time to think of anything else.

3 THUNDER OVER THE SCHOOLROOM

Annie called her little squirrel Scamper because he moved so fast. At first she kept him in a box in her room and fed him milk, or cornmeal mixed with cream. Soon he was big enough to eat hickory nuts that she cracked for him.

Spec didn't like Scamper. He would walk around the box and sniff at him. Then Spec would go off and lie down with his head on his paws and watch the box with distrustful eyes.

Annie worried about Spec and Scamper. But one day she discovered that she didn't need to worry anymore. It had been a cold night, and when Annie woke up she found that Scamper had crawled out of his box and curled up against Spec to keep warm. They were friends after that. Annie's troubles were over, but Amanda's troubles were doubled.

"Animals sleeping on the floor!" she would say. "Squirrels scootin' up the bedposts! Laws-a-massy, it just ain't fittin'. That's what."

One day, the breeze was blowing in fresh off the river. The sun was beating down on Arlington with all the warmth of summer. Amanda was up early. This was just the day she had been waiting for to air all the blankets out in the sun—beautiful, heavy blankets that had been hand-woven in the spinning house from wool clipped from Grandpa Custis' own sheep.

Amanda went in and out of the house quietly with the bedding. Robert Lee was also at work in the library, which opened off of the big dining room at the south end of the house. When he moved into Arlington House, he took over the responsibility of managing the great estate. It included a thousand sheep and hundreds of acres of tobacco, fields of grain, and vegetable patches. He had to work early mornings and late at night on his books because his work at the army engineer's office in Washington took up most of his days.

Boo and Fitzhugh were with him. Their father insisted that they learn how to manage the farm as part of their education. The sheep meant wool and meat and leather and glue and tallow for the family and for the market. The production of these things was a whole industry in itself.

Tobacco raising was a science. It took more than

countless field hands to produce a good crop. The boys were learning from their father when the plants should be "topped." The small blossoms had to be picked to make the tobacco leaves grow better. They learned how to cultivate the young plants and guard against disease. They learned to recognize the mottled green and yellow leaves that were ripe for picking. They learned how to hang the ripe leaves in ventilated sheds to dry. Growing tobacco was another great industry.

"When I wasn't much older than you are, Fitz-hugh," said his father, who was sitting at his big desk with his dark head bent over his account book, "I was the man of the house. I learned the value of money at an early age, and I insist that you boys learn something about it, too."

"Yes, sir."

Mr. Lee added up a long column of figures and wrote down the sum with his quill pen. Then he went on:

"We had to leave our big plantation, Stratford Hall, and live in a small house that my mother owned in Alexandria." He made a few notes on the margin of the page about the cost of seed. The boys were familiar with the house in Alexandria he mentioned.

"My father seemed to have bad luck wherever money was concerned. Don't misunderstand me, he was a fine gentleman—distinguished himself under

General Washington during the revolution. He was known as Light Horse Harry Lee—high courage—splendid fellow."

The boys stood quietly waiting for him to go on.

"There are two things I want you to remember."

"Yes, sir."

"Always spend a little less than you have and keep the esteem of your friends. Remember this, and half the battle of being a success and a gentleman is won."

"Yes, sir."

By seven o'clock Amanda's blankets were blowing in the sun. They were her pride and joy. She would sun them well and pack them away in the linen room at the end of the upstairs hall until winter.

Amanda came in through the conservatory. It was time to go up and help Annie get ready for breakfast.

In Annie's room Scamper was in a playful mood. He ran in and out between Annie's feet as she washed her face in the washbasin on the stand. When Amanda came into the room, Scamper ran up her calico skirt as quick as a flash. He dashed around her dark neck on his little prickling claws and climbed up onto the top of her white bandanna. By digging his claws in sharply, he used the top of Amanda's head for a springboard. He took off, soared through the air, and landed on the top of the bedpost.

Amanda screamed loud enough to wake everybody from Arlington to Alexandria. She snatched the bed warmer off its hook at the side of the fireplace and went after the squirrel. Around the house they went, down the back stairs and up the front.

Amanda was chasing Scamper. Spec was chasing Amanda, and making no secret of it. Annie was chasing Spec. Down through the front hall they went like bedlam let loose. Finally Scamper escaped through the front door, ran through the rose garden, and vanished into the dark forest.

"Hm!" said Amanda setting her bandanna straight and smoothing down her skirt. "That squirrel ain't no more'n a second cousin to a chipmouse. That's what. Chipmouses can't run around on my head. No, ma'am! Good mornin' Mr. Lee."

"What's going on out here?" demanded Robert Lee sternly as he came out into the hall.

"He's gone!" cried Annie.

"Who's gone?"

"Scamper. He ran out the door and into the woods."

"Never mind, Goldilocks, he'll be back. He's getting pretty big you know. He's entitled to the freedom of the outdoors just as you are. He'll be back when he wants some food. You better run up and brush your hair; here comes our breakfast."

The trays of food began arriving from the summer kitchen. Grandma and Grandpa Custis came down. Aunt Lucy came down with Millie in her arms and holding Bob by the hand. There was no company in the great house this morning, so the family ate their breakfast in the small family dining room. Spec curled up under the table near Bob's place, waiting for his crop of crumbs.

"By the way, Amanda," said Robert Lee, "a bed warmer is not considered the best weapon for hunting small game."

"No, sir."

Boo laughed and choked on a piece of ham.

"And another thing, Amanda."

"Yes, sir."

"Mrs. Lee has a touch of the rheumatism this morning. She is not coming down for breakfast. See that a tray is sent up to her."

"Yes, sir."

"She wants you to take charge in the schoolroom this morning. She can't give the children their lessons as she usually does."

"I can't even read or write, you know that," said Amanda.

"You stay there and keep an eye on them. Let them work by themselves."

"Your horse is ready, sir," said Uncle Daniel at the door.

Robert Lee finished his breakfast. He said goodbye to all the children — Boo, Fitzhugh, Mary, Annie, Agnes, Bob, and Millie — and left to ride across the long bridge to Washington to work.

After breakfast Amanda gathered the children in the schoolroom. The windows were open that morning, admitting the lazy song of the bullfrog in the creek, the song of the thrush in the holly tree, the fragrance of the rose garden, and the soft warm air. The children could hear the remote voice of Aunt Lucy who was out on the grass under the trees with Agnes, Bob, and Millie. The schoolroom seemed very small and confining.

Mary sat down to work on a piece of lace that she was making. Boo and Fitzhugh slumped lazily in their chairs with the mathematics chart between them.

Neither of them was thinking about twice times twelve or the area of a square. Both of them were thinking about the news they had heard that morning: Captain Donahue's *Bonnie Bristol* had been sighted sailing up the river toward Alexandria. Both of them were thinking about their small boat moored in the creek. If they could start in time, they might be able to sail to meet the *Bonnie Bristol*.

Annie found her story of *Hansel and Gretel* that she had been reading. She thumbed through it and found her place.

"Now you just read out loud to me," said Amanda. "Then I'm sure you are working like you should." She settled herself comfortably in a rocker and folded her hands.

Annie took one last look outdoors to see if Scamper was in sight, and then she began:

"Hansel and Gretel were lost in the woods. They came to a candy house——"

"You sure it says that right on the paper there?" asked Amanda.

"That's what it says." Annie went on:

" 'Let's take a little bite,' said Hansel.

'Who's nibbling at my house?' said a gruff voice, and the ugly old witch opened the door and asked them in.

The fire was burning brightly on her hearth. The old witch licked her lips and thought, 'Little girl, you are plump and tender. You will make me a fine dinner.' Then she sang:

'Hocus and pocus and cranberry jell,
Hop in the oven and sit for a spell.'

'Not I,' said Gretel, 'I don't know how to hop in an oven.'

Then the old witch sang:

'Hocus and pocus and hinges that creak.
Open the oven and just take a peek.'

'Not I,' said Gretel. 'I don't know how to open an oven.'

'Stupid,' said the old witch. She was getting impatient for her dinner. She sang:

'Hocus and pocus and sparrows and crows,
Open it this way and stand on your toes.'

And the ugly old witch lost her balance and fell into the oven. Hansel and Gretel were saved."

Amanda's eyes were popping out of her head. She was so busy listening to Annie read that she didn't notice what the boys were doing.

Boo had quietly left the room, and Fitzhugh was looking intently out of the window at the sky.

"Why are you standing by the window, Mister Fitzhugh?" asked Amanda.

"Think it's clouding up a little. Looks like it might rain."

"Nonsense, child," said Amanda. Then she thought of her blankets on the line. "What's that you say?"

There was a long, low rumble overhead.

"Thunder," said Fitzhugh.

Amanda heaved herself out of the rocking chair and peered at the sky. As she did so, Boo, who had gone up to Annie's room, rolled an old cannonball across the floor again.

"Thunder!" said Amanda, and without another word she swept out of the room to rescue the blankets. School was over for the day.

4 PIRATE'S PRIZE

The children were out of the schoolroom and running down the hill toward the creek in a flash. Boo and Mary and Fitzhugh were sprinting like deer. Annie could hardly keep up with them. Her legs in her ruffled pantalets fairly flew. She hadn't forgotten Scamper. She kept looking around for him as she ran. Finally she tripped over a root and fell down flat, scratching her nose and tearing the hem of her dress.

"Better look where you're going when you run downhill," advised Fitzhugh.

Boo came back and brushed off her skirt.

"Where are we going?" asked Annie blinking back the tears.

"Sailing down the Potomac in our boat. We're going to try to meet the *Bonnie Bristol*."

"In the storm?"

Boo laughed. "There isn't a hatful of wind or a drop of rain in that storm. Come on Annie, we have to hurry."

Annie ran on down the hill with them, her heart pounding. She wasn't often included in the high adventure of her older brothers and sister.

"I told Uncle Daniel to meet us at Alexandria, at Jones' wharf with the coach," said Boo, "and I got some food from Uncle Ephraim for our lunch."

"Alexandria!" thought Annie. "That's five miles down the river. A real trip. Anything might happen."

The little boat was a flat-bottomed scow that the boys had made out of planks cut from one of the pine trees in the dark forest. It was their pride and joy.

They all climbed in and shoved off. They paddled it down the creek and out into the open water of the river. They hoisted the old linen sheet that served as a sail. They were off to meet Captain Donahue. With the help of a favorable wind and the current of the river, they moved slowly toward their destination.

Before the great, white pillars of Arlington were out of sight, they opened their lunch. Uncle Ephraim had packed corn bread, thick slices of ham, cold turkey, hard-boiled eggs, and some little cakes. Nothing had ever tasted better.

The brackish tidewater of the river brought with

it the smell of the open ocean, of seaweed and shellfish.

"Let's pretend we're pirates sailing out from Spain," said Annie.

"Let's," said Mary, and she shaded her eyes with her hand and looked all around. "Not a sail on the horizon," she said.

The little boat drifted slowly along. Boo almost went to sleep at the tiller. There was no sound but the lap of the bow wave and the slap of the lines against the sail.

"A ship, a ship!" cried Annie, who was keeping a sharp lookout.

"Sit down," said Fitzhugh, "and don't let your imagination run away with you."

Annie was quiet for a minute. Then she said in a little voice, "But I saw a ship."

Boo sat up and shaded his eyes. "She's right. The ship is in. Captain Donahue has just dropped his canvas and tied up at Jones' wharf. It's the *Bonnie Bristol* all right."

"I believe you're right," said Fitzhugh. "A fair prize indeed. All hands on deck! Man the guns! Stand by to board her from windward side."

The *Bonnie Bristol* tied up at Alexandria about twice a year. It was always an exciting occasion for the Lee children and the whole Lee family. An English ship was a market for the products of the farm. It was news from the outside world. It was a visit from a friend.

The little boat moved along down the river, nearer and nearer to Alexandria. When Boo tried to head in toward the great hull of the *Bonnie Bristol*, he found that the current of the river was stronger than the wind. No matter how he turned his rudder and trimmed his sail, the little boat went straight on down the middle of the Potomac.

"I can see men running around on the deck," said Mary.

"Certainly," said Fitzhugh. "They're unloading."

"I think we are outnumbered," said Annie, still playing pirate.

"You aren't going to be scared are you," said Boo, "like a little sister?"

"Hey," yelled Fitzhugh when he saw they were drifting on past the landing, "where are you going?"

"Stand by to drop the sail," replied Boo. "We'll have to row."

"Annie and I will row," volunteered Mary as she sat down with Annie on the middle thwart.

Mary dug her oar into the water and pulled on it, half spinning the little boat around.

"Come on, Annie, you must row, too. Like this." Mary took another stroke.

Annie felt the oar heavy in her hand. She tried to dip it in the water and pull against it as Mary did, but all she managed to do was scoop up about a bucketful of the Potomac and splash Boo with it from head to foot.

"Say," gasped Boo when he could get his breath. "That's no way to row!"

Annie tried it again. She dug her oar in deeper this time. She pulled with such force that she lost her balance and fell over backward into the bottom of the boat.

The little boat shot forward and whammed into the weathered planking of the stout hull of the *Bonnie Bristol.* All of them were pitched off their seats with the jolt.

A whiskered Captain Donahue leaned over the deck rail, twenty feet above the water, and looked down.

"What have we here?" he asked.

"Pirates," shouted Annie, picking herself up. "Stand by to be boarded!"

Captain Donahue threw back his head and roared with laughter. "Well, if it isn't the Lee children," he said. Then he dropped a rope ladder over the side for them; he made the top of it fast to the deck railing. The loose end of the rope ladder whipped in the wind in a most elusive manner.

Boo stood up and caught the bottom rung and held it steady.

"You first," he said to Annie.

"Me?" said Annie swallowing hard.

"Well," said Boo, "real pirates would probably use grappling hooks to hold the boats together. Then they would swing across from one to the other on the rigging—with a cutlass in their teeth."

"Very well," said Annie, taking a deep breath, "I'll climb the rope ladder, but hang onto it and hold it steady."

Each rope rung of the ladder collapsed around her foot as she stepped on it, giving her a feeling of questionable security. The coarse rope cut into her hands, she hung on so tightly. Finally she reached the top, and Captain Donahue helped her over the rail. Mary followed her, and then Fitzhugh and Boo.

Soon they were all standing in that enchanting world of lines and boat gear—the afterdeck of a sailing vessel.

"Now, I'm not much of a prize," said Captain Donahue. "But I would be glad to be taken prisoner to Arlington—that is, if you still serve baked ham and hot biscuits like the ones I had the last time I was there." His round, jovial face had the weather-beaten look of a Yorkshire pudding, and it was framed in sandy hair and whiskers.

"We do indeed, sir," said Boo. "You must come with us."

"Quite so."

"I asked Uncle Daniel to meet us here with the coach so that we could get to Arlington as soon as possible," Boo added. "Are you ready to go now, sir? Uncle Daniel will be right along, I am sure."

Annie had taken hold of the great wheel that was as broad as she could reach. She pretended she was the helmsman, steering the boat by stars and compass across the world and back again.

"Just a minute," said the Captain, "you pirates can't go home empty-handed." He disappeared below and returned in a few minutes with several packages. "I have some presents here for your lovely mother, some blue silk and some tea and some of His Majesty's spices." The Captain had stopped while he was below and put on his blue captain's coat with its brass buttons and his skipper's hat.

They all started across the gangplank to the wharf just as the coach appeared, rocking along over the cobblestones toward them. Uncle Daniel was resplendent in his bright red coachman's coat and his gray plush hat a foot high. Amanda sat on the high seat beside him, hanging onto the iron rail with one hand and onto her bandanna with the other.

The minute the coach stopped, she climbed down from her high seat and swooped down on the children like a hawk on a brood of chickens.

"Miss Annie, you don't belong down here without somebody to look after you. Don't you know that?"

"She has a man to look after her, you know," said Boo stepping up.

"Two men," added Fitzhugh, pulling himself up as tall as he could.

"Just the same, it ain't fittin'! That's what it ain't." She took Annie firmly by the hand and led her toward the coach. "Look at your dress. And what you been doin' to your nose?"

The boys went back to get their little boat and tied it up to the wharf until they could come back for it. Then the four children and Captain Donahue climbed into the coach. Amanda picked up her yellow skirt and climbed up over the wheel to her high seat beside Uncle Daniel. Uncle Daniel cracked his whip, and they went rolling back along the cobblestones of Alexandria.

Amanda smoothed down her "ruffled feathers" as they went along. She had the Lee children under her hand again, at least temporarily.

Soon they left the town behind them and were riding along the wooded road that wound its way to the great house at Arlington.

"I think Amanda is right," said Boo. "You really aren't quite big enough to do the things the rest of us do, Annie."

"You splash when you row."

"You fell off the seat."

"You better stay home and play with Angelina, your doll."

"Mamma wants to teach you to sew."

They didn't mean to be unkind, but Annie huddled in the corner of the seat and was utterly miserable.

"Never mind," said Captain Donahue, "you'll jolly well grow up someday and show them all how to do things. And don't you feel bad about falling off that seat. Why, the last time I was over here my little dog—one of the smartest in the world—fell clean off the boat into the river. I never saw him again."

"Spec!" thought Annie. "Why, Spec is his dog, of course." It was perfectly clear to her. She opened her mouth to speak, but she couldn't make a sound. Her throat felt as though she had swallowed one of the oars.

"Tell us about your trip across the Atlantic, Captain," said Boo.

The Captain began to tell them of his stormy sea voyage. He was still talking when the coach rolled up to the front door at Arlington.

Amanda climbed down and went to the summer kitchen. Mrs. Lee would want a duck roasted or a wild turkey, and one of the finest hams, and lots of hot breads for her friend, the Captain.

The children ran up the steps and into the house.

"Who is there?" called their mother from the drawing room.

"Pirates," shouted Boo. "A whole pirate crew with a fair-sized prize and some booty."

5 WHOSE DOG ART THOU?

Annie went straight to her room. There was warm water in the big blue-and-white pitcher on the stand. She poured some into the washbowl and scrubbed her face until it shone.

She looked over the dresses in her closet. Finally she chose a dimity with tiny sprigs on it and a ruffle that came to her ankles. It was a very special occasion when Captain Donahue came to Arlington. There would be good things to eat, and talk of the sea, and news from England, and bargaining for the tobacco crop. She put on her best black slippers.

Annie hadn't seen Spec since she came home. Perhaps he had gone off to the field where the sheep were pastured. Perhaps he was chasing rabbits in the dark forest. Perhaps he wasn't Captain Donahue's dog, after all. Perhaps he had been trying to swim across the river when her father found him. All these thoughts danced through her head as she buckled her slippers.

Down in her heart Annie knew that Spec was the Captain's dog. She would have to tell him sooner or later that she thought so. Boo and Fitz-hugh and Mary must think so, too. Not one of them had said a word about it in the coach coming home, but they would expect her to tell him herself. That she knew.

She started down the steps slowly. She wouldn't have to tell him until after dinner. There couldn't be any harm in that.

Annie went into the drawing room where the family was listening to the Captain's story of his trip across the ocean. Her mother sat with the heavy folds of the blue silk across her lap.

This hour in the drawing room before supper was one of the happiest of the day. Robert Lee had come home from Washington, and all the children were there. The conversation was gay and sprinkled with laughter.

Annie sat down on a little stool near the dining room door. She was starving. It had been hours since they had eaten their lunch out in the little boat.

She could see the big table in the dining room. There was a bowl of magnolia blossoms in the center, and the tall silver candelabra shone.

Finally, the great trays of food began to arrive from the summer kitchen, and Mose came to the drawing room door to announce that supper was ready.

Aunt Lucy took the three smaller children, who had already been fed, off to bed. Tonight Annie was allowed to eat with the grown-ups.

"This is the first good meal I've seen in ten weeks," said Captain Donahue.

"And we've kept you waiting too long. You must be starved," said Robert Lee.

"I won't be hungry much longer," said the Captain, taking his place.

Boo held his mother's chair for her. Fitzhugh held Mary's. Annie started to pull out her own chair, but her father was there in a twinkling to help her. He seated her as graciously as he would any great Virginia beauty.

"Thank you," she said, smiling up at him. She glowed with the thought that she was almost a lady. But she was still something of a pirate, too. When Mose appeared at her elbow with a platter of roasted wild turkey, the pirate in her won out. She had some wild grape jelly, and some baked ham and some greens and some hot bread.

It was some time before her mind came back to Spec. But when it did she lost her enthusiasm for the dessert. Annie excused herself and left the table. She must find her dog and break the news to him. She must tell Spec the Captain was back.

She went along the driveway and looked in the spinning house. She went to the summer kitchen, one of Spec's favorite spots in all of Arlington. She stopped at Aunt Lucy's quarters, and at Uncle Daniel's. Spec wasn't there.

She began to be a little alarmed. She ran through the rose garden to the stable. But Spec wasn't there. She called him and called him.

Finally she heard a little whimpering noise and she saw Spec sitting under a tree.

"What's the matter with you?" said Annie. "Don't you know I've been looking and looking for you?"

Spec sat under the tree without moving. He cocked his head to one side and looked up in the tree.

Annie came up to him, and then she saw Scamper. The little squirrel was trying to build a nest. He would bring a green leaf to the crotch of the tree. Then while he went after another, the leaf would blow away.

"Poor little thing," said Annie. "You want to build a nest and you don't know how. You will fall out if you try to sleep in that one. You better let me help you."

Annie ran back to the summer kitchen and got a little wooden pail.

"Where are you going with that thing?" asked Fitzhugh.

"I'm going to build a nest for Scamper up in the big oak beyond the stable."

"Well, you're all dressed up. You can't climb a tree. I'll help you."

Fitzhugh wedged the wooden pail into the crotch of the tree. Then he filled it with leaves. They watched for a few minutes. Scamper came to it, sniffed it, and jumped into it.

"I can bring him nuts everyday," said Annie.

"You better," said Fitzhugh, "or he'll come to the house after them himself."

They walked along through the rose garden in silence for a minute. Then Fitzhugh said:

"Papa told Captain Donahue about Spec."

"Oh," said Annie. "I was going to tell him myself when I got back."

"I know."

They came around the house to where Captain Donahue and Robert Lee were smoking their after-dinner cigars and enjoying the view across the river.

Spec sniffed at the Captain's long legs for a minute. Then he yelped and jumped on him in great excitement.

"Well, well, well!" said the Captain. "You haven't forgotten me, have you old chap?" He roughhoused with Spec for a minute. Then he turned to Annie.

"Your father has told me what fine care you have taken of my little dog."

Annie smiled a little. She was thinking: "It will be lonesome without him sleeping by my fire on winter nights."

"He's a great dog," laughed the Captain, "always ready for fun. Oh, and that reminds me. I brought over a game from England that I want to give you to show my gratitude for the care you have given this little fellow."

He disappeared into the house a minute and came out with a package.

"These are shuttlecocks," he said.

"What kind of cocks, sir?" asked Annie.

"A shuttlecock is a piece of cork with feathers around it. These are the rackets. You bat the cock back and forth and if you let it touch the ground you lose a point. We call it Battledore and Shut-tlecock. Great game. Everyone is playing it in England."

Annie picked up a shuttlecock and tried to hit it with the racket. It looked simple. She felt silly batting at the empty air as the cock fluttered to the ground. She tried again, but Spec got in her way.

Spec! Spec would be going away.... The Captain hit a cock to her and she returned it.... He won't be bothering Amanda anymore, or tracking mud into the hall, or getting dog hairs on the rag rugs.

He won't be coming home to me with burrs in his coat. He won't sit under the table at my feet as quiet as a mouse. He won't be going with me on picnics to the spring. . . . She tripped over Spec and missed the cock.

"That's a point for me!" said the Captain. "You will soon learn to play. Nothing to it, after you practice a bit."

Annie sat down on the grass and gathered Spec up in her lap.

"You must be very careful," she said to him, "not to fall off the boat again. You would drown before they could turn that big thing around and go back to pick you up. Anyway, if you're going to be a sailor you might as well be a good one. Good ones don't fall off the boat, you know."

Spec reached up and licked her ear.

"And don't eat anything that will make you sick. Sweet potatoes, especially. Maybe the Captain will let you sleep on the foot of his bunk so you won't catch cold."

Captain Donahue dropped down on the grass at her side.

"I'm afraid I'm a bit stupid. I'm not thinking of taking that dog with me. Not for a minute. Aboard ship is no place for a dog when he can have a home like this and someone to love him."

Annie buried her head against Spec's neck because she was ashamed of her tears.

"I never had a thought of taking that dog away from here. . . . I hope the shuttlecocks will repay you for all the trouble he is to you."

"Oh, he isn't any trouble, really," said Annie.

"Good. Then I will come around to see him every time I get to America, if I may."

"Please do," said Annie. And she put her arms around Captain Donahue's neck and cried freely down into his collar.

6 FOUR-FOOTED QUEEN OF HALLOWEEN

Fall came to Arlington. The dark forest turned red and yellow. Pumpkins ripened into balls of gold in the fields. The apples hung red on the trees.

Everyday the boys went out to hunt wild turkeys. Hickory logs were stacked near the back door, ready to feed the hungry fireplaces of the great house.

Uncle Ephraim moved in from the summer kitchen to the winter kitchen, which was in the basement of the house below the schoolroom.

All hands were busy storing food for the winter. The smokehouse was hung so full of hams and sides of bacon and turkeys that the heavy door fairly bulged on its hinges.

The best apples were packed in barrels and put in the storeroom. The rest of them were put through a cider press. Carrots, beets, parsnips, and turnips were buried in a bin of sand.

Wagonloads of corn and wheat were hauled across the long bridge and up along the canal to the mill at Georgetown. They came back as bags of flour and meal.

The kitchen with its big open fireplace and its big brick ovens was fragrant with the spicy smell of apple butter and chili sauce.

The Lee children had to spend every morning in the schoolroom, but they were free in the afternoons. One afternoon Annie appeared at the kitchen door with a pumpkin under each arm.

"I bet a tomato to a jar of jam you want me to bake a pumpkin pie," said Uncle Ephraim. He was standing over a great iron kettle stirring pudding with a long wooden spoon.

Annie stood looking thoughtfully at him for a minute. Then she said, "If you just had some long, stringy hair and a hat, you could be the witch."

"I could be a which?"

"A witch! You know—ride a broomstick and stir a brew."

"Bless my soul and sauces, it ain't Halloween again, is it?"

"That's what it is."

"Well!" Uncle Ephraim moved his kettle to a trammel at the side of the fire so the contents wouldn't burn. "That bein' the honest truth, we better get to carvin' those pumpkin faces quicker'n a cat can twink a whisker."

He got out his knife and sharpened it. Then he sat down at one of the long wooden tables and went to work. Annie leaned on her elbows and watched him, entranced. Uncle Ephraim was an artist. Under his nimble fingers, corn-silk hair grew on the pumpkin's yellow skull; a carrot nose hooked down over a red-pepper mouth. Turnip ears protruded from the side of his head. Small disks of red apple glared at you from the eye sockets.

Annie clapped her hands with delight. Uncle Ephraim put an old straw hat on Mr. Pumpkin and called him finished. Mrs. Pumpkin turned out just as ugly, in a more refined way. When her small sunbonnet was tied in place, she was ready to take

her place with Mr. Pumpkin in the center of the table in the big dining room.

Annie carefully carried them off to the dining room. In a minute she was back with a little pumpkin about the size of a big tomato.

"Uncle Ephraim, don't you think Millie and Bob and Agnes should have a pumpkin on their table, too? They don't eat in the big dining room, you know."

"I suspect you don't eat in there yourself," said Uncle Ephraim.

"I can eat in the big dining room tonight, because some cousins are coming, and we are going to celebrate Halloween."

The little pumpkin came to life in Uncle Ephraim's hands. Soon it was grinning at Annie with its funny little face.

"Thank you. Thank you so much," said Annie, running off with it.

Soon Boo and Fitzhugh began bringing wooden buckets of water from the well and filling the washtubs back of the chimney in the kitchen.

"Why are you bringing water in at this time of day?" said Uncle Ephraim.

"We're going to duck for apples after supper," said Fitzhugh. "Halloween, you know."

"I know about that. What I can't figure out is how I'm going to turn out a supper with all you children takin' over my place of business."

Later that afternoon, a carriage rolled up to the door and five or six young people piled out and came into the house. After the excitement of the greetings was over and it quieted down so Robert Lee could get in a word, he said:

"Children, this is Halloween. Ghosts walk in the dark of the moon. Witches ride through the night on their broomsticks. Black cats cross your path on silent feet. I will give you all one hour to dress the part of Halloween. Come down before supper in your costume. The best one will get a prize."

They all fled. Except for an occasional snicker from the second floor, the house was quiet for an hour while each of them worked out a costume to fit the day.

Boo appeared first, a scarecrow with straw sticking out of his sleeves and his neck and the top of his hat. Fitzhugh and Mary came as a pair of ghosts with sheets around them. One of the cousins strung corncobs together and wore them like the bones of a skeleton. One of the boys came in with a long piece of chain clanking at his heels.

One of the girls had made herself a little hat out of oak leaves and wore a long necklace of acorns. Annie couldn't think of a Halloween costume for a long time. Finally she saw one of her mother's big, black shawls. She put it around her shoulders, held out her arms, and called herself a bat.

Robert Lee looked them all over. He walked up

and down the hall trying to decide who should have the prize. He liked the oak leaf hat and the necklace. He thought the skeleton of corncobs very clever. Boo was a perfect scarecrow. He slowly looked them over, trying to pick a winner.

Before he could make a decision, the most peculiar creature ever seen at Arlington, or anywhere else, came scooting down the hall.

The creature had a small body, about two hands high as you measure a horse. It had a long bushy tail, a striped fur coat, and a round, yellow head that wagged frantically from side to side and grinned at everybody.

The girls squealed and jumped back against the wall in astonishment. The scarecrow stepped on the chain and tripped the boy who had it fastened to his ankle. The skeleton was so alarmed his corncob bones all bumped together in his haste to get out of the way and give the strange creature the center of the hall. Robert Lee laughed at all of them.

"The cat!" cried Annie. "The poor cat. Here kitty, here kitty, you need some help." She knelt on the floor and helped the cat get the pumpkin off her head. Agnes and Bob had left their little pumpkin on a chair and the curious cat had put her head into it and couldn't get it out. They all laughed to think how alarmed they had been.

"That settles it," said Robert Lee to the laughing children. "The cat wins the prize for the best Halloween costume. She shall have a saucer of cream for her supper. The rest of you runners-up can divide the box of maple sugar candies."

"Hurray for the queen of Halloween!" said Fitzhugh, and they all trooped into the dining room.

They had a yellow supper of cornmeal mush and mashed rutabagas and pumpkin pie. Then after supper they all filed down to the kitchen below the schoolroom to duck for apples in the big wooden tubs. The great fireplace in the middle of the room divided the kitchen from the laundry. Its roaring fire threw flickering shadows on the whitewashed walls.

Mary got an apple on the first try. Boo and Fitzhugh each ducked for one. Both came up with their heads dripping and bright red apples held firmly in their teeth, looking for all the world like a pair of water spaniels that had retrieved a couple of balls.

Most of the guests managed to capture an apple after a few tries. Finally it was Annie's turn. She

wanted, so much, to get an apple in her teeth as the others had done. She was surprised to find the apples so big and round and hard. Every time she tried to dig her teeth into one it would shoot away to the bottom of the tub in a most elusive manner.

But Annie was determined. She stood on her tiptoes and leaned over the side of the tub with the business-like air of a turtle who has his eye on a fly. She snapped at the apple and her teeth closed on it, but she lost her balance and plunged head-first into the enormous tub. She was draped, limply, over the side of the tub like a wet shirt that is waiting to be wrung out and hung on the line.

Fitzhugh grabbed her by the waist and set her on her feet, dripping.

"I got it," said Annie back in her throat as she grinned around the apple in her teeth. But the party was all over for her in spite of her small success.

Amanda bundled her off up the back stairs to her room and rubbed her down before the fire with a big towel. She gave Annie a dose of Dr. Taylor's Extract of Liverwort to keep her from catching cold and bundled her into bed.

Spec settled down before the fire with his head on his paws. Amanda snorted at him and left the room. She thought she heard Annie sniffle just a little. She wasn't sure whether the child was crying softly to herself or whether it was just because her yellow hair was spread out damp on the pillow.

7 ANNIE AND THE WOODEN SKATES

Winter settled down on Arlington shutting them off for weeks at a time from the rest of the world. The children, however, were never at a loss for something to do. They lived in a gay and busy world of their own making. A relatively small world it was, and full of trouble for Amanda.

"I don't know what you want these for," said Amanda one day, gingerly holding up a pair of wooden skates as though they were a couple of fish of questionable age. It was a cold day and the wind howled around the corner of the house. The fire crackling on the hearth was reflected in the polished walnut of the bedroom furniture.

Annie was listening to neither Amanda nor the winter wind. She was perched on the top of her feather bed, an elf on a haystack, pulling on her woolen stockings.

"Haven't you got about everything a child could want, without these?"

There was no answer. Annie was having a little difficulty with the woolen stockings.

"Your mamma's took to her bed with the rheumatiz, and your papa most likely can't get home 'cause of the snow. No ma'am, it ain't fittin' for you to go risking your neck on these contraptions. Not fittin', that's what. Everything's all wrong when a gal takes to skate slidin' by herself. You're fixin' to get yourself in trouble."

"Look, Amanda!" said Annie as she looked out her window. "Look! The wind has almost swept the ice clean. It's beautiful."

The Potomac, which cut through the white hills below the house like a dark ribbon, seldom froze over. But there was a little creek which flowed into it which did. Now it was a clear sheet of ice, sparkling in the sun.

Amanda tried again. "Your pony, Santa Anna, needs to be rode. Or maybe you could ride Creole?"

"Mary has gone off on Creole."

"Well, where are Boo and Fitzhugh?"

"Hunting rabbits."

"You wouldn't like to crack hickory nuts for the cake, Miss Annie?"

"No."

"You could help Mose make the candles."

"No." Annie jumped down off the bed scorning the little wooden steps and shook out her rumpled skirts.

"I'm going skating," she announced, as though Amanda had never suspected it.

"These skates is Mister Fitzhugh's, you remembers that," warned Amanda.

"I know, but Boo made them. He makes everything. They won't care if I just try them."

"You're treadin' on the patience of the Lord!" said Amanda, summing up the whole business in one snort. She swept out of the room to go down and vent her ill temper on the biscuit batter.

Annie tied on her bonnet securely and tiptoed down the long stairway.

All of the children at Arlington lived an exciting, adventurous life, but Annie couldn't always keep up with the others. She couldn't ride very well. She had let Creole throw her at the jump. She used an oar like a scoop shovel. She wanted to try skating. She thought perhaps she could do that and keep up with the others. But she wanted to try it alone. She was proud.

She picked her way down the steep embankment to the river. She followed the river to where the frozen creek joined it. It was a friendly, singing river in the summer, but now, up close, it seemed dark and threatening. Spec followed at her heels.

Once in awhile he would sniff at an inviting rabbit trail. But he always came back to Annie.

Annie glanced up at the house. The great white pillars seemed to frown down at her. The wind caught her scarf and whipped it against her face. She felt lonely and a little frightened.

She finally reached the stretch of ice and sat down on a log to put on the skates. She worked fast to buckle them to her high-button shoes. They were much too long for her little feet. The wooden ends stuck out forward and curled up toward her chin.

She stood up and slid out on the ice. But something was wrong with her ankles. They turned in.

She straightened up and slid farther out on the ice feeling more and more insecure every inch of the way. Her ankles turned out.

Despair closed in around her heart. She would never, never be able to do all the things the other children did. Her legs weren't any good. Her ankles wouldn't work. They seemed to be made of rags and rubber. They ached clear up above her shoetops. The frowning house seemed miles away. Annie felt very alone.

Suddenly a gust of wind caught her. It bellied out her full skirts into a sail and carried her down the clear, windswept ice toward the open water of the river. She couldn't catch her breath. Her cheeks tingled with cold and her nose felt blue.

With a supreme effort she steered her wabbling

ankles toward a snowbank at the river's edge. Unable to stop herself, Annie fell headlong into it.

The snowbank felt soft and safe. But Spec was barking like mad and dancing around her, and she knew she couldn't stay there. She sat up, dug the snow out of her neck, and unbuckled the skates. She tried her ankles carefully to see if they could be counted on to carry her home. They could, and Annie started back to the house.

"Never," thought Annie, "will I try to skate again. I will listen to Amanda. I just can't do things. I'll stay at home and learn to cross-stitch, and dip candles, and crack nuts." Heavyhearted with discouragement she plowed her way home through the snow.

8 ANNIE FINDS THE ANSWER

"Well, if you aren't one of the worst lookin' sights I can call to mind!" said Amanda when Annie came in the back door. "You get yourself upstairs and into some dry clothes before I can turn this hoecake!"

Annie sadly tiptoed up the back stairs. Spec, his tail between his legs, followed. Annie wiped the skates carefully and put them back in the playroom. Then she went into her own room, changed into dry clothes. Then she went down to the drawing room.

Her mother was there in a chair with a shawl around her shoulders. And her father was home! He had been all the way to Baltimore, but he had come home. It took more than a few snowdrifts and a cold wind to keep him away. Fires roared in both of the fireplaces of the enormous room and the brass fenders shone.

The warmth and friendliness of that huge room reached out and enfolded her in a soft embrace. Here was comfort and love, security from wind and weather, and rest for weary ankles. And her father was home. Everything took on a different color for Annie when her father was home.

She rushed across the room and flung her arms around his neck. She wouldn't ask him what he had brought her. He would tell her after awhile.

"What have you been doing these days I've been away, Boo?" said Robert Lee to his oldest son as he settled down in a Windsor chair and took Annie on his lap.

"The most interesting thing I did was to make a steel plow."

"A steel plow?"

"Yes. Some fellow named Deere made one out in Illinois and it works. I wanted to try it."

"Hm," said his father, "you *are* an engineer, son. And the man who builds a better plow for his country builds for peace."

There was a lull in the conversation.

"Now," thought Annie. "Now he will tell me."

"Well?" said her father, holding her off at arm's length to look at her affectionately.

"A blue teapot?" ventured Annie.

"I brought you a teapot last week, silly."

"A yellow cat?"

"You have eleven cats, already. Or is it twelve?"

"A dog?"

"There's Spec, you know. You wouldn't want him jealous, would you?"

"Papa tell me, tell me," she threw her arms around his neck.

"Well then, little Buttercup, look in that basket over by the door."

Annie flew over and brought the covered basket back to the fire and opened it carefully. It might be a yellow kitten, or a chipmunk, or a baby squirrel.

She peeked in and the color drained out of her face and landed in the pit of her stomach. There in the basket was a beautiful pair of wooden skates.

Skate! She could never skate again.

She smiled and kept the tears from swelling over. One didn't cry and say, "I can't"—not when one's great grandfather was George Washington.

"Thank you, Papa," she said, smiling.

"You like them?"

"They are beautiful."

"I tell you what we'll do," said Robert Lee bursting with enthusiasm, "the first thing tomorrow morning we'll go down to the creek and skate together. Skating—great sport—makes the blood tingle through your veins. Fun, too. You wait and see."

"Yes, Papa," said Annie. She put the skates back in the basket. She knew about skating. It wasn't any fun if you couldn't do it. It wasn't any fun if your ankles didn't work.

Supper was announced and the family went into the candle-lit dining room. Annie tried to eat, but she couldn't swallow her baked chicken and her corn bread over the lump in her throat.

Early the next morning her father stuck his head in her door and said: "Good morning, Bluebell. Don't forget we're going skating after breakfast. Skating will put roses in your cheeks."

Annie was silent at breakfast. She knew what it would be like. She knew she would disappoint him again. He wanted her strong and active like the rest, and loved her particularly because she wasn't.

She climbed the stairs to her room to get ready. Reluctantly she pulled on her heavy stockings. "I won't tell him I can't do it," she thought. "He would laugh and say, 'Nonsense, Tiddledeewink.' I won't say I can't do it. No, Papa wouldn't like that. I don't care how hard it is. I'll have to do the best I can for him."

She buttoned her high shoes. Then she took her heavy coat off the nail in the closet. Slowly she buttoned it and tied her scarf around her neck.

"I'll go and try to skate," she said to herself, "then he'll see. I'll be another disappointment to him, that's all."

She pulled on her mittens. She was ready. She looked around her cosy room with its glowing fire, reluctant to leave its warmth and comfort. Sadly she turned and went down the stairs. Her father was waiting for her in the hall.

The two of them went down the hill to the creek. It was a clear, sparkling day. The snow was downy soft under their feet.

Annie sat down on the log. Robert Lee knelt before her and buckled on the new wooden skates.

She was surprised at the way they fit. They were the same size as her shoes. The wooden ends curled up just a little as they should. Her father had buckled them on her securely. Then he put on Fitzhugh's skates, and they were ready.

Annie stood up and threw an appealing look toward her father. She would like, just for once, not to be a disappointment. In a minute he would know that she couldn't skate any better than she could do anything else.

Annie's father came over and took hold of her

two hands and skated out on the ice with her. Her ankles were not so bad. They just turned in.

"Now," said her father, "bend forward just a little and push off with your right foot. That's it. Now your left. Get some force into it."

Annie, supported by her father, began to skate with regular strokes. Her spirits rose. She could learn. It just took her longer, maybe. She grinned up at him.

"Fun isn't it, Toodletoes?"

"Most fun I ever had," said Annie. The color flamed up in her cheeks. She glowed. She worked at getting long smooth strokes with a determination that would have pleased George Washington himself. She pushed off with her left foot, then her right. The support in her father's strong arms gave her confidence. She looked up at him, furtively. Why, he wasn't disappointed at all. He was having fun.

They skated in silence for a minute. Then Annie said: "I was just thinking——" They were sailing down the ice with the wind off the river tingling against their faces.

"Yes?"

"I was just thinking, that everything is all right when somebody loves you, isn't it?"

"Funnyfeather, I believe you're right," said Robert E. Lee. He twirled his little daughter around, and together they skated back toward Arlington House.